# Faultergeist

*Faultergeist (n.): A ghostly presence that represents moments of hesitation or doubt.*

# Faultergeist

Nikhil Kunche

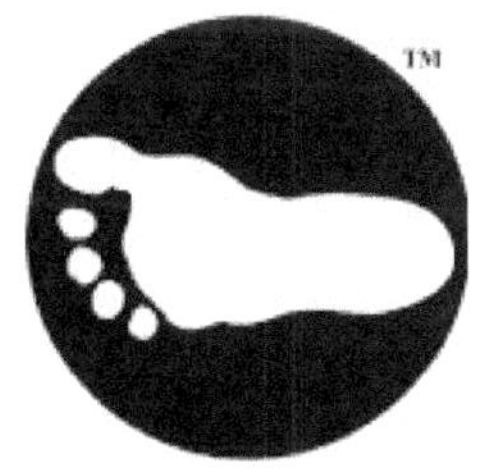

Bigfoot Publications

*Because, there's a writer in everyone.*

**Faultergeist**
**Author : Nikhil Kunche**

**First Published by**
Bigfoot06 Publications (OPC) Pvt. Ltd.
1st floor, BSR Building near Vishal Mega Mart,
Daultabad Flyover, Laxman Vihar Phase 3,
Gurugram, Haryana (122001)
Website: www.bigfootpublications.in
Email: info@bigfootpublications.in

**First Edition : October,  2023**
**© Nikhil Kunche**

ISBN Print Book -  978-81-19512-90-4



Typeset in Palatino Linotype 11pt
by Yachika Prajapati For Bigfoot06 Publications

Printed in India

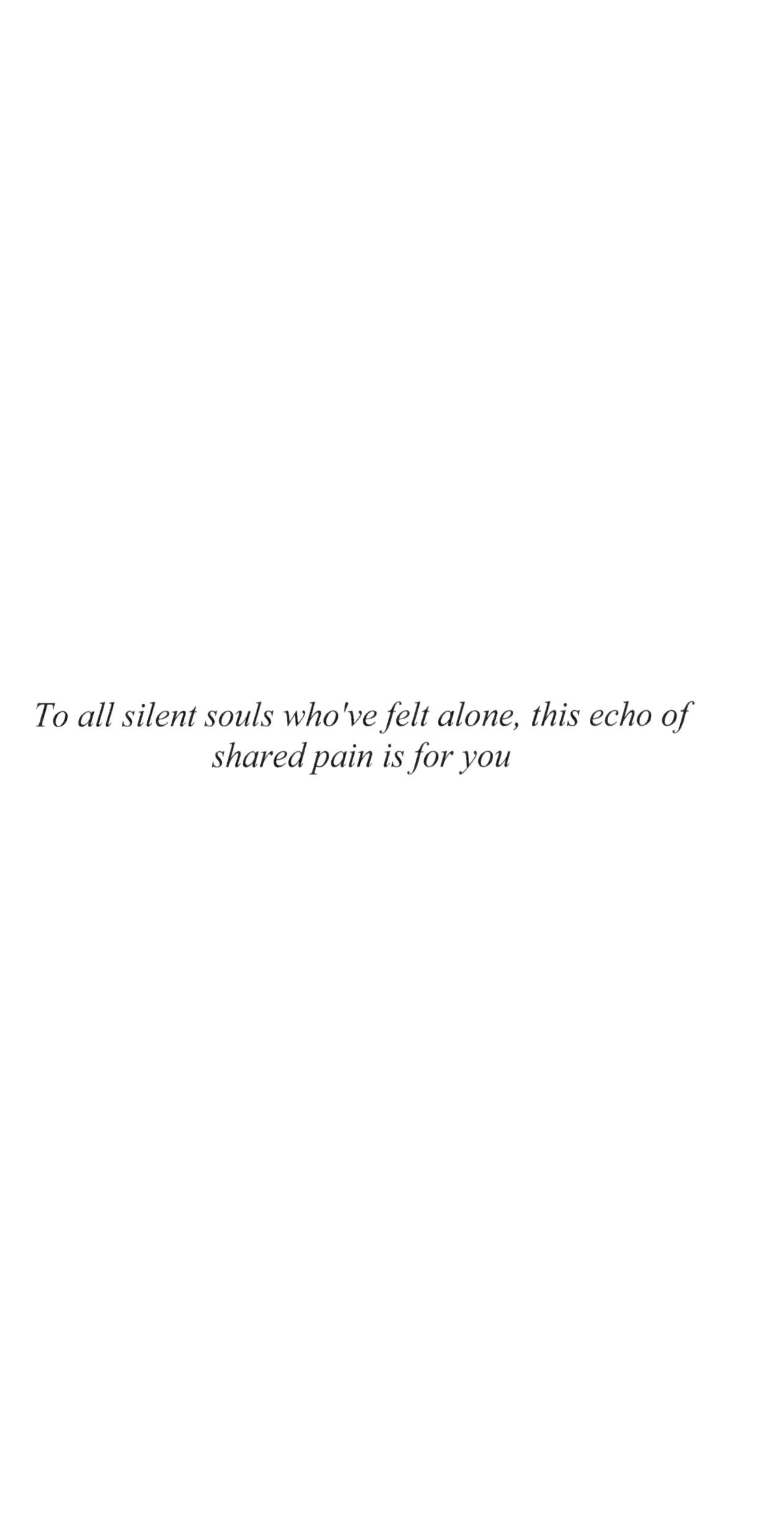

*To all silent souls who've felt alone, this echo of
shared pain is for you*

# PREFACE

Life, in all its myriad complexities, offers a spectrum of experiences. Some moments are radiant, casting a luminous glow, while others are shrouded in shadows, echoing with silent cries. This collection of poems is a tribute to those muted voices, to the souls who've felt the weight of the world pressing down on them, yet have persisted.

Each verse is a reflection of raw emotions, of struggles and triumphs, of despair and hope. They are born from personal experiences, yet they resonate universally, touching the chords of countless hearts that have known pain and yearning. This anthology is not just a journey through the valleys of solitude and peaks of longing but also a testament to the resilience of the human spirit.

To the reader, I hope these poems offer solace, a sense of camaraderie, and perhaps a gentle reminder that even in our loneliest moments, we are never truly alone. Through these lines, may you find a mirror to your own experiences and the strength to voice the unspoken.

*With heartfelt sincerity,*
*Nikhil Kunche*

# TABLE OF CONTENTS

# Solitude's Silken Cradle

Amidst the chorus of joyous spree,
A lone shadow lingered, silent as the sea.
While jubilant voices filled the ground,
His quiet heart echoed not a sound.

Sunlight kissed faces, leaving a golden hue,
But his world was painted in a sombre blue.
Every gesture, every muted plea,
Echoed a wish, to simply be free.

The playground's rhythm, a symphony so sweet,
But his heart drummed a different beat.
While castles of joy rose from the ground,
His fortress of isolation was all he found.

The faultergeists, with their mocking tone,
Whispered, "In this vastness, you're all alone."
They circled, their shadows dark and long,
Feeding his fears, singing their haunting song.

In life's grand mosaic, vibrant and wide,
He felt like a smudge, always set aside.
Dreams were his refuge, a realm apart,
Where hope could gently cradle his heart.

Trees shared tales with those who listened close,
But to him, they stood silent, almost morose.
Winds brought stories from distant shores,
Yet in his world, they closed all doors.

A relentless tide of desolation he bore,
In a cacophonous world, he was the silent core.
Others danced in life's radiant beam,
He remained adrift, lost in a dream.

The faultergeists revelled in their cruel game,
"Look, young lad, no one knows your name."
Yet, a spark within refused to die,
A flicker of hope, reaching for the sky.

To speak the tongue of shared smiles,
To traverse friendship's boundless miles.
But chains of solitude, cold and stark,
Kept him ensnared, in perpetual dark.

The world spun on, not missing a beat,
He felt like a shadow, incomplete.
Yet in stories, in verses bold and true,
He sought a world, where he could be anew.

"Is there a place, a moment to be?"
The haunting refrain, a constant decree.
In life's vast play, with roles so diverse,
He felt adrift, lost in the universe.

But a glint of promise, distant and fine,
Whispered of a day, when stars would align.
For now, he wandered, seeking a ray,
Believing in dawn, after the darkest day.

In "Cradled Solitude", a narrative begins,
Of a soul, its battles, and silent wins.
A tale of resilience, in shadows cast,
A spirit undeterred, by its troubled past.

# Echoes of Elusive Play

Schoolyard tales of joy and chase,
Children united, setting the pace.
But where joyous voices intertwined,
One lad lingered, always behind.

The games went on, the children played,
In the midst of it all, his hope began to fade.
While others were chosen, embraced, and sought,
He was left behind, an afterthought.

His heart ached, watching from the side,
A silent observer, his pain he'd hide.
The joy of camaraderie, the thrill of the chase,
Seemed forever out of his embrace.

In the quiet corners, he'd often sit,
Pondering the puzzle, trying to fit.
"Why am I different? Why am I shunned?
Is there a flaw, or something I've done?"

He'd watch the shadows grow long and thin,
As the sun set, and evening would begin.
The weight of solitude, heavy and profound,
Yet, in his heart, resilience was found.

For in the silence, a voice did speak,
Whispering of strength, when one feels weak.
The journey ahead, filled with unknowns,
But he'd face it bravely, forging his own stones.

And as days turned to nights, and nights to days,
The boy learned to navigate life's intricate maze.
Though the playground's memories lingered, bittersweet,
He stepped forward, refusing to accept defeat.

For the next chapter awaited, with lessons anew,
Promising experiences, perspectives to view.
The boy, now stronger, would face each test,
With the wisdom of the past, and hope in his chest.

# Hushed Halls of Hidden Hopes

Between the walls where lessons took flight,
Ancient tales whispered, fading with the night.
Shadowed alcoves held silent lore,
Of a youth, whose journey many chose to ignore.

He walked the corridors, head held low,
Past lockers and classrooms, in a rhythm slow.
Yet, behind closed doors and shadowed nooks,
Were whispers about him, inquisitive looks.

"Have you heard?" one would say,
About the boy who seems lost, day by day.
"He's different," another would claim,
Assigning him labels, without a name.

The weight of words, unseen but felt,
Beneath their pressure, his spirit would melt.
Yet, no one dared to approach or ask,
Behind the facade, the boy's true task.

He yearned for connection, a genuine bond,
Not just fleeting glances or a wave from beyond.
But the whispers grew louder, a cacophonous din,
Drowning his thoughts, the turmoil within.

Yet amidst the noise, a realization did dawn,
That he wasn't alone at the break of the morn.
For many hid their stories, their pain, their strife,
Behind masks of normalcy, leading a double life.

With newfound clarity, he began to see,
The power of empathy, the key to be free.
For while whispers might wound, and rumours might sting,
True strength lay in the lessons they bring.

And as he journeyed on, through life's intricate dance,
He vowed to give every soul a fair chance.
To listen, to understand, to truly perceive,
The stories untold, the webs we weave.

# Bruised Knees, Empty Benches

Upon the field where aspirations soared,
Where victories were cheered, and defeats mourned,
A lone figure gazed, passion in his gaze,
Chasing dreams, through life's intricate maze.

He watched the others, swift and agile,
Their laughter echoing, mile after mile.
In games of chase, of ball, of might,
He wished to join, to share the light.

But every attempt, every outstretched hand,
Met with mockery, a line in the sand.
For every dive, every sprint, every leap,
Ended in falls, wounds cut deep.

The benches bore witness to his silent plea,
As he nursed his bruises, by the old oak tree.
"Why am I different? Why can't I blend?"
He'd often ponder, seeking an end.

Yet, with every fall, a resilience grew,
A determination, strong and true.
For he realized, in pain's harsh glow,
That failure was merely a way to grow.

The empty benches, once a symbol of despair,
Became his sanctuary, a space of repair.
Where he'd strategize, plan, and train,
To face the morrow, come sun or rain.

And as days turned to weeks, and weeks to years,
The boy's efforts quelled his initial fears.
For he learned that success isn't just in the win,
But in the journey, the effort, the fight from within.

Though the playground battles were tough and grim,
They prepared him for life, made him strong in limb.
For in the school of hard knocks, he earned his degree,
A master of endurance, as strong as can be.

# Chalked Chronicles of Transience

Once bright-eyed, eager to learn and explore,
Now burdened by numbers, scores that bore.
Each mark on the board, each grade on the sheet,
Felt like chains, pulling him off his feet.

The weight of expectations, the pressure to excel,
Turned vibrant subjects into a personal hell.
Math's intricate dance, science's wondrous song,
Now felt like paths where he didn't belong.

Whispers echoed, "He's not the brightest, you see,"
As he grappled with concepts, longing to be free.
But within those walls, amidst the fading chalk,
A silent rebellion began to walk.

He sought knowledge, not for grades or acclaim,
But to quench his thirst, to douse the flame.
He delved into books, not in the curriculum set,
Finding solace in stories, a safety net.

For in the tales of old, and legends of yore,
He found heroes who too, were scored less, ignored.
Yet, they rose, with passion, with a drive,
Their stories taught him to thrive.

The fading chalk marks, once a source of dread,
Became mere numbers, as he surged ahead.
For he realized, true learning isn't in the score,
But in the quest for knowledge, the desire for more.

And as the years passed, and the chalk marks faded,
His love for learning never once abated.
For he knew, in life's grand, vast arc,
It's the journey that matters, not the final mark.

# Teacher's Blind Spot

Where intellects flourish and ideas combine,
Amongst budding scholars, one failed to align.
A young soul, overshadowed, adrift in the sea,
His presence felt, yet as silent as it can be.

Teachers with wisdom, guiding the flock,
Yet, to this boy, they seldom did talk.
He'd raise his hand, hope in his eyes,
But was often overlooked, to his surprise.

Not the star pupil, nor the troublemaker,
He existed in between, a silent undertaker.
Of lessons unlearned, of praises unsaid,
He tread the middle path, with quiet dread.

In the bustling classroom, a world of its own,
He felt like an island, utterly alone.
Questions bubbled, doubts did sprout,
But fear of ignorance kept them from coming out.

Yet, in the shadows, away from the spotlight's glare,
He nurtured a flame, with tender care.
A passion for subjects, not taught in class,
He ventured into realms, where few would pass.

While teachers remained blind to his silent quest,
He dove into books, giving his best.
Finding mentors in authors, guidance in prose,
He built his sanctuary, where knowledge flows.

And though in school, he remained unseen,
In the world of ideas, he was a king, not a teen.
For every teacher's blind spot, every overlooked soul,
Holds a universe within, a story untold.

In time, some educators did realize,
The depth in his questions, the spark in his eyes.
But whether seen or unseen in that school's plot,
He continued his journey, needing validation or not.

# Dawning Horizons

Between changing scenes and evolving days,
The lad discovered paths in life's intricate maze.
New terrains whispered, both broad and wide,
Offering a haven from memories he wished to hide.

No longer confined by memories of old,
He ventured forth, brave and bold.
New faces, new voices, a fresh start,
Hoping for acceptance, he played his part.

The air was different, the vibe so new,
A chance to rewrite, to misconceptions bid adieu.
He observed the cliques, the laughter, the jest,
Wondering if here, he could finally rest.

In this newfound realm, friendships blossomed slow,
Tentative connections began to grow.
Shared interests, mutual respect, trust earned,
For the first time, he felt the warmth he yearned.

Yet, amidst the joy, old fears did linger,
Memories of isolation, like a ghostly finger,
Touched his heart, made him doubt,
Would this new world too, cast him out?

But as days turned to weeks, and weeks to months,
He found his tribe, shared lunches and stunts.
Laughter echoed, secrets were shared,
In this new haven, he felt truly cared.

The horizon that once seemed distant and cold,
Now painted stories, vibrant and bold.
For in this chapter, the lad did find,
A place where he wasn't left behind.

# Serenades of Secluded Balconies

In the quiet of twilight, beneath a silvered moon,
The lad glimpsed a vision, a heart's sweet tune.
Adjacent balconies, a stage for silent plays,
Where glances exchanged held stories, a secret maze.

She, a beacon of grace, with eyes that sparkled bright,
He, a silent admirer, lost in the gentle light.
Their worlds apart, yet so close in space,
A dance of eyes, a delicate chase.

The wind carried whispers, soft melodies of the heart,
Each stolen glance, an unspoken work of art.
Butterflies fluttered, a sensation so profound,
In this silent ballet, emotions unbound.

Why did she smile? Why did she stay?
In the theater of balconies, what role did he play?
Questions swirled, as he dared to dream,
Of shared moments, and what they might deem.

A snow globe, a token, a gesture so raw,
Held hopes and dreams, without a flaw.
Delivered with trembling hands, a message enclosed,
A heart's confession, feelings exposed.

Yet, fate's cruel jest, a twist unforeseen,
Shattered the dream, the space between.
Rejection's sting, sharp and clear,
Yet the balcony tales, he'd forever hold dear.

For in those silent exchanges, a lesson was learned,
Of love's fleeting dance, and the hope that burned.
Though paths diverged, memories remained,
Of balcony serenades, and a love unexplained.

# Glass Globe Reverie

Within the world of whispered wishes and sighs,
The lad cradled a sphere, reflecting the skies.
A glistening orb, with a winter's embrace,
Marking a moment, a tender heart's grace

He'd offered his heart, encased in that sphere,
Hoping it'd bridge the distance, draw her near.
But the world is vast, and dreams often shatter,
Leaving behind fragments, of what truly matter.

The globe, once a beacon, now lay cracked,
Echoing the pain, the courage he lacked.
For in its fragile form, a truth was sealed,
Of vulnerabilities exposed, emotions revealed.

Yet, within the shards, a glimmer did gleam,
For every broken dream births another dream.
Though the globe was fractured, its essence was true,
A testament to feelings, deep and anew.

The lad learned of risks, of wearing one's heart,
Of the beauty in beginnings, and the pain when they part.
But with every ending, a new chapter does start,
In the glass globe reverie, he found his art.

For life isn't about the dreams that break,
But the courage to dream, the chances we take.
And so, with hope in his eyes, and love in his core,
The lad ventured forth, to dream once more.

# Corridors of Concealed Cries

Between age-old walls, where wisdom's tales are spun,
Through corridors echoing, walked the forlorn one.
In search of meaning, through heartache's shadowed lanes,
In academic pathways, where life's rhythm remains.

The weight of the past, on his shoulders did press,
Yet, new horizons beckoned, a chance to redress.
Amidst lectures and lessons, he sought to impress,
But memories of rejection, his heart did distress.

In the crowd, he'd wander, a face among many,
Seeking solace in books, yet finding not any.
For the whispers of past, were louder than any lecture,
Echoing the pain, of every past fracture.

Yet, amidst the despair, a glimmer did shine,
For college was more than just a line.
It was a place of rebirth, of starting anew,
A chance to find oneself, to one's essence be true.

In quiet corners, he'd pen down his fears,
In the library's silence, shed hidden tears.
But with every tear shed, strength he did find,
To face the world, with a determined mind.

For college wasn't just about grades or degrees,
It was about finding oneself, amidst life's vast seas.
And as he walked those corridors, with hope in his stride,
He learned to face life, with his heart open wide.

# Alchemy's Airy Appetite

In a world of laughter, music, and dance,
Friends gathered, leaving none to chance.
Yet, in the midst of joy and revelry,
One was forgotten, left to his solitary.

Homebound, with hunger as my guide,
An empty kitchen, my spirit's slide.
Despair took hold, a walk I sought,
Yet nature's tears, another battle fought.

Racing to shelter, beneath a tree I stood,
Its droplets mocking, my somber mood.
I cursed its branches, its leaves so green,
Yet envied its secret, a magic unseen.

For in its silence, a marvel it spun,
From air and sunlight, its feast begun.
Colors and flavors, from simple delight,
A bounty of nature, in every bite.

Anger turned to wonder, as I delved deep,
Into nature's kitchen, its secrets to keep.
Artificial photosynthesis, the term I found,
A promise of sustenance, from air all around.

Imagine a world, where hunger's no more,
Where food from thin air, is not just lore.
A dream ignited, from a night so bleak,
In the heart of despair, a purpose I seek.

For in the darkest moments, when all seems lost,
Nature whispers secrets, at no great cost.
From a tree's simple magic, to mankind's great quest,
In the alchemy of desolation, hope finds its rest.

# Duplicity's Embrace

In the dance of life, where trust is the tune,
He stepped with hope, under the bright moon.
But shadows lurked, even in daylight's boon,
For betrayal's sting, would pierce him soon.

He held close those, he thought were dear,
Shared his dreams, his joys, his fear.
But in the mirror of trust, cracks did appear,
As duplicity's embrace, drew eerily near.

A friend's mask, worn with practiced ease,
Hid intentions dark, like a disease.
Promises made, were but a tease,
As behind his back, they did as they please.

The sting of betrayal, sharp and deep,
Made him question, the company he'd keep.
For in the world's vast, tumultuous sweep,
Not all that glitters, is gold to reap.

Yet, from the ashes of trust once burned,
A valuable lesson, he discerned.
Not all are worthy, of the trust earned,
And by duplicity's hand, many are turned.

But with resilience, he chose to rise,
Wiping away, the tears from his eyes.
For in life's vast, ever-changing skies,
The truest strength, in oneself lies.

# Dreams in Digital Dalliance

Digital landscapes beckoned, intricate and profound,
He navigated pathways, where dreams were unbound.
Between bits and bytes, he sought his stride,
Where hopes could flourish, or be denied.

With fingers dancing on keys, a rhythm so true,
He crafted visions, in shades of binary hue.
A gateway for payments, seamless and free,
A dream that could change commerce's decree.

But as codes intertwined, and algorithms spun,
The weight of the past, again begun.
Memories of betrayal, of love turned sour,
Haunted his hours, stole his power.

The digital realm, with its endless scope,
Promised escape, offered hope.
But shadows of real-life, with its pain and strife,
Crept into his code, disrupted his life.

A missed semicolon, a glitch in the script,
His ambitious project, suddenly slipped.
Errors piled on, like relentless waves,
Drowning his dreams, in digital graves.

Yet, amidst the chaos, a beacon did shine,
A reminder of days, when all was fine.
The support of friends, from school days of yore,
Their faith in him, made his spirit soar.

With renewed Vigor, he tackled the code,
Correcting each error, lightening the load.
For in this digital realm, he began to see,
A reflection of life, and what could be.

Challenges would arise, both old and new,
But with perseverance, he'd see them through.
For dreams, though deferred, never truly die,
They await their moment, to once again fly.

And as the sun dawned on a new digital day,
His gateway was ready, come what may.
A testament to resilience, to dreams held dear,
In the digital realm, he conquered his fear.

# Affection's Anchored Albatross

City streets echoed memories, both old and new,
He treaded paths, reflecting on the life he once knew.
Love held him close, yet chains did bind,
Family's embrace, both a blessing and bind.

The house that once echoed with laughter and song,
Now felt like a cage, where dreams didn't belong.
Love was abundant, care never did lack,
But freedom's sweet taste, he yearned to have back.

His mother's gentle voice, a lullaby so sweet,
Yet her words of caution, made his heart skip a beat.
"Don't venture too far, stay close to the nest,
For in our embrace, you'll always find rest."

His father's strong hands, that once lifted him high,
Now held him grounded, under the same sky.
"Traditions are important, they define who we are,
Don't chase fleeting dreams, or you'll drift too far."

Siblings, with whom he'd played, fought, and grown,
Now had lives of their own, dreams of their own.
Yet, in their concern, in their protective gaze,
He felt the weight of the past, the pull of old days.

He loved them dearly, this he couldn't deny,
But the chains of affection made him often sigh.
For with every step towards his dreams, so bold,
He felt the tug, the urge to fit the mold.

In the silent nights, when the world was at bay,
He'd gaze at the stars, and silently pray.
For strength to balance, love with ambition,
To honour his roots, yet fulfil his mission.

For family is precious, a treasure so rare,
Their love and concern, beyond compare.
But the heart has its calling, a song of its own,
A melody that beckons, to the unknown.

And so, in the dance of love and dreams,
He sought a balance, a middle it seems.
For in the chains of affection, he began to see,
Not just confinement, but strength, the key.

The key to endure, to rise, to soar,
With the winds of ambition, to explore.
For family's love, though binding it seems,
Is the anchor that grounds, even the wildest dreams.

# Divergent Dialogues of the Deep

Among the stars and the cosmic dance,
He sought life's rhythm, its profound trance.
Galaxies whirled, mysteries unfurled,
His journey for purpose in the world swirled.

Books stacked high, ancient tomes and scrolls,
Seeking answers, he delved deep into their folds.
Philosophers of old, their thoughts profound,
Yet, in their wisdom, clarity he rarely found.

Socrates questioned, Nietzsche proclaimed,
Kant's critiques, Descartes' mind games.
From Eastern Zen to Western existentialism,
He waded through theories, seeking a prism.

A prism to refract life's myriad hues,
To understand pain, joy, the daily news.
Why do we suffer? Why do we strive?
What's the point of being alive?

He debated with scholars, argued with priests,
From grand cathedrals to spiritual feasts.
Yet, every answer led to more queries,
Life's maze seemed a series of theories.

In coffee shops, under dimmed lights,
He discussed life, its wrongs and rights.
With intellectuals, artists, and the common man,
He sought a universal, encompassing plan.

But with every discourse, every heated debate,
He felt more lost, entangled in fate.
For every philosophy, every belief he'd find,
Contradicted another, played tricks on his mind.

Then, in the quiet of a starlit night,
A realization dawned, clear and bright.
Perhaps life's meaning wasn't set in stone,
But something each must find on their own.

No book, no theory, no sage could impart,
The answers he sought, deep in his heart.
For life's true meaning, its essence so fine,
Is a personal journey, a unique design.

And so, with renewed Vigor, he chose to explore,
Not just the world, but his core, evermore.
For in seeking answers outside, wide and far,
He'd forgotten the answers lie in who we are.

# Lenses, Lies, and Lustrous Lives

As neon lights danced and screens came alive,
He yearned for recognition, a chance to thrive.
Through the lens, moments frozen in time,
Yet the soul behind, remained a silent chime.

The camera's gaze, unflinching, stark,
Captured his essence, both light and dark.
Each click, each flash, left its mark,
But the fleeting praise, was but a lark.

For in the age of digital acclaim,
Where likes and shares, were the ultimate aim,
He found himself, in a relentless game,
Chasing validation, in fame's fickle frame.

Every pose, every smile, meticulously planned,
Hoping to be noticed, to be grand.
Yet amidst the applause, he'd often stand,
Feeling hollow, on shifting sand.

The world saw the facade, the external sheen,
But the struggles within, remained unseen.
For every picture-perfect scene,
Lay countless moments, that had been.

Behind the filters, the edits, the hue,
Lay a story, raw and true.
Of battles fought, of challenges anew,

Of moments of despair, and breakthroughs too.
Yet, the world's attention, ever so brief,
Moved on swiftly, leaving behind grief.
For in the vast digital reef,
He was but a leaf, seeking relief.

The weight of expectations, heavy to bear,
As he constantly sought, to compare.
His worth, his value, in a digital square,
Where numbers dictated, if one was rare.

But with time, a realization did dawn,
That true worth, wasn't externally drawn.
For the camera's gaze, and the world's fawn,
Were transient, and soon would be gone.

He chose to detach, from the digital race,
Seeking solace, in a quieter space.
Where self-worth wasn't a chase,
And life wasn't confined, to a digital base.

For beyond the camera, beyond the screen,
Lay a world, vibrant and unseen.
Where moments were felt, not just seen,
And where he could truly, be serene.

# Wings Waxed by Waiting

Beneath the endless stretch of blue,
Where hopes soared and dreams grew,
He remained anchored, with a vision true,
Bound by chains only he knew.

The horizon beckoned, vast and wide,
Promising adventures, worlds untried.
Yet familial chains, side by side,
Held him back, his dreams denied.

The weight of expectations, heavy and real,
Dictated his path, his every deal.
The dreams he harboured, the zeal he'd feel,
Were often met with a cautionary spiel.

"Stay close to home, don't venture far,
The world's a storm, you're but a star.
Seek not the unknown, bear no scar,
For in our midst, you'll surely spar."

Yet within him, a fire did burn,
A restless urge, a yearn to turn
Towards the unknown, to discern,
The lessons life had, at every churn.

He'd watch the birds, soaring high,
Unfettered, kissing the sky.
And wonder why he couldn't try,
To break free, to amplify.

The world outside, vast and grand,
Held mysteries, in every land.
Yet he was stuck, in familiar sand,
His dreams and hopes, forever banned.

But time, the great healer, did impart,
A wisdom deep, a change of heart.
For he realized, he could start,
A journey within, an inner art.

While external flights might be restrained,
His inner world remained unchained.
There, his dreams and hopes remained,
Untouched, unmarred, unstained.

He dove deep, into his soul's core,
Discovering realms, never seen before.
Realizing that there's so much more,
To life, to dreams, to explore.

And so, while the world saw him stay,
In familiar grounds, day by day,
He travelled far, in his own way,
In the realms of his mind, come what may.

For true freedom, he came to see,
Wasn't just about breaking free.
It was about understanding, the key,
That within oneself, one could always be.

# Compliance's Crafted Cage

Among the murmurs and veiled glances,
Where society sets rigid stances,
He moved, a silhouette, yielding to each demand,
Every obligation an unyielding hand.

The world demanded, and he complied,
His dreams and desires, cast aside.
For the happiness of others, he bore the weight,
Yet, in the depths of night, he'd contemplate.

"Why do I silence my heart's true song?
Why do I constantly go along?
With every demand, every plea,
Why can't I just let myself be?"

But the chains of compliance held him tight,
Every "yes" a link, every "no" a respite slight.
The world praised his selflessness, his grace,
Unaware of the tears that marred his face.

# Tattooed Promises

Through urban streets, where lanterns cast a sheen,
He journeyed, chasing visions yet unseen.
The murmur of crowds, the night's mystic call,
Offered transient joys, a respite from all.

Tattoo parlours with their buzzing needles,
Whispered of commitments, as fragile as rose petals.
He watched as ink etched stories on skin,
Permanent reminders of places they've been.

A name, a date, a symbol, a sign,
Each tattoo a testament, a love's design.
He remembered her, the one who wore his name,
Inked on her wrist, a burning flame.

But as time passed, the ink did fade,
Just like the promises, they both had made.
The love that once felt eternal and true,
Became a ghost, a shade of blue.

Yet, in the midst of the city's din,
He sought another, to begin again.
A new promise, a fresh start,
Hoping to mend his fractured heart.

He met eyes that sparkled, lips that smiled,
Promises whispered, emotions dialed.
But deep down, a fear did reside,
Would this too, be a fleeting tide?

For in the world of tattooed vows,
Promises are as transient as the night allows.
Yet, he hoped, amidst the city's maze,
To find a love, that truly stays.

But as dawn approached, and the night did wane,
He realized the cycle, the recurring pain.
For in the realm of inked desires,
Burned the remnants of forgotten fires.

# Desires Dancing on Deserted Dunes

Across the heart's shifting sands and tunes,
Desires ebb and flow, beneath moons.
Guided by destiny's unpredictable gait,
They Mold the path, through love and hate.

Once, as a child, desires were simple and few,
A toy, a friend, skies endlessly blue.
But as the sands shifted, and years did pass,
Desires grew complex, like shadows on glass.

In the fervour of youth, ambitions took flight,
Dreams of success, shining so bright.
The heart yearned for love, passion, and fame,
Each gust of wind, fanning the flame.

But with age, those flames began to wane,
Replaced by desires, more subtle, yet plain.
A moment of peace, a loved one's embrace,
The simple joys, life's hectic pace often erase.

Yet, amidst the swirling sands of desire's play,
Some wishes remain constant, come what may.
The need to be seen, to be understood,
To find a place in the world, where one truly could.

But often, the winds of life are unkind,
Leaving behind desires, unfulfilled, maligned.
Yet, hope persists, in the heart's deep core,
For winds change direction, bringing desires once more.

As the twilight of life approaches, slow and sure,
Desires become memories, pure and pure.
The winds may have scattered many a dream,
But the heart holds close, those that truly gleam.

In the end, as the final grains of sand drift away,
It's not the desires, but the journey that holds sway.
For in the dance of windswept desires and dreams,
Life finds its rhythm, in endless streams.

# Twilight Conversations

As twilight settled and shadows grew long,
He pondered in silence, where he belonged.
The fading glow, the day's final song,
Signalled time's passage, relentless and strong.

With every dusk, memories would play,
Of laughter, tears, and the light of day.
Conversations with himself, deep and profound,
Seeking answers, to life's mysteries unbound.

Why was he here? What was his role?
Questions that weighed on his soul.
The pain of the past, the hope for tomorrow,
Twilight brought both joy and sorrow.

In the hush of the evening, he'd often find,
Whispers of yesteryears, flooding his mind.
The times he felt lost, the moments of glee,
All came rushing back, like waves of the sea.

He'd ponder on choices, the paths he'd tread,
The words left unsaid, the tears he'd shed.
Yet, amidst the introspection, a realization grew,
Each experience, each trial, had his spirit renew.

For in these twilight conversations, wisdom took flight,
Guiding him gently, through the darkest night.
Embracing the lessons, the pain, and the strife,
He found solace, purpose, and the essence of life.

And as stars began to twinkle, in the vast expanse above,
He felt a connection, a universe of love.
For in the silence of twilight, he came to see,
The beauty of existence, and all it could be.

# The Weight of Silent Sacrifices

Upon life's grand stage, where facades often sway,
He acted his part, day after day.
Yet deep within, hidden from the fray,
Were silent burdens he bore, come what may.

Every nod, every agreement, every smile,
Hid a story of compromise, mile after mile.
For in his quest to make others content,
He ignored his needs, his voice went silent.

The world lauded his generosity, his kind soul,
Unaware of the toll it took, the gaping hole.
For not being able to say "no" was his greatest pain,
A self-inflicted wound, a never-healing strain.

Yet, amidst the applause and the cheers,
He yearned for someone to see his silent tears.
For while the world celebrated his selfless art,
Only he knew the true cost, the breaking of his heart.

# Sands that Sing of Shifts and Shadows

In a land where golden dunes rise,
Underneath the cerulean skies,
He ventured forth, with hope in his eyes,
Seeking himself, amidst the desert's ties.

The scorching sun, relentless and fierce,
Burned his skin, made his vision pierce.
Yet, in this vastness, something did coerce,
A quest for identity, a universe to traverse.

Foreign tongues, unfamiliar chants,
Intricate patterns, cultural grants.
He treaded softly, took cautious glances,
Learning the rhythm, the desert's dances.

The mirages beckoned, illusions so sweet,
Promising solace from the relentless heat.
Yet, he knew they were but deceit,
False hopes that would retreat.

Loneliness engulfed, vast and profound,
In this barren land, no soul around.
Yet, whispers of the past did resound,
Echoes of memories, tightly bound.

The shifting sands, ever so sly,
Changed paths, made him retry.
Yet, with every step, he'd sigh,
For amidst the change, his spirit did fly.
Nights brought solace, a starry embrace,
Cool winds, a gentle grace.
Under the canopy, he'd trace,
Dreams of home, a familiar place.

Yet, amidst the isolation, he found,
A strength within, a connection unbound.
For even in desolation, life did surround,
In every grain of sand, life did resound.

The desert, with its trials and tests,
Taught him resilience, no time for rests.
For in its vastness, he found quests,
Challenges that put him to the best.

And as the days turned into years,
He shed his doubts, overcame his fears.
For the desert, with its joys and tears,
Shaped his identity, crystal clear.

In the dance of winds and golden grains,
He found his purpose, broke his chains.
For amidst the desert's gains and pains,
He discovered himself, and his own lanes.

# Shadows of Regret

Within the quiet vaults where memories sleep,
Echoes of the past begin to seep.
Choices once made, now casting a shade,
Of love unclaimed and moments betrayed.

Once, in the brilliance of youth's glowing sun,
Decisions were made, actions begun.
With the confidence of invincibility's embrace,
Steps were taken, in life's relentless race.

But as the path twisted, turned, and wound,
Some choices led to pain profound.
Words spoken in anger, love unreturned,
Opportunities missed, bridges burned.

In the quiet of night, when the world's asleep,
Those shadows emerge, making the heart weep.
Whispers of what could've been, had one known,
Echoes of laughter, love, now forever gone.

Yet, amidst the weight of regret's heavy chain,
Emerges a truth, clear and plain.
Each shadow, each sorrow, each tear,
Has shaped the journey, year by year.

For in the dance of light and dark,
Life finds its rhythm, its unique mark.
Regrets may linger, casting shadows long,
But they're but notes in life's ongoing song.

With the wisdom of years, one comes to see,
That regrets, though painful, set the soul free.
For in acknowledging mistakes, in facing the night,
One finds the strength, to seek the light.

And as the journey continues, with its ups and downs,
The heart learns to smile, more than it frowns.
For in the dance of shadows and the sun's golden ray,
Life's true beauty is revealed, in a myriad display.

# Verses Veiled in Raven's Riddle

In the stillness of a moonlit night,
A raven perched, black as the void, yet bright.
Its eyes, deep wells of ancient lore,
Held tales untold, of yore and more.

"Who are you?" the man dared to ask,
Seeking solace from his weary task.
The raven tilted its head, a gesture slight,
And began its tale, taking flight.

"I am the messenger, the keeper of tales,
I've seen kingdoms rise, I've seen them fail.
I've witnessed love, I've seen despair,
I've been to realms, few ever dare."

The man, intrigued, drew closer still,
Hoping the raven's words would fill,
The void within, the questions vast,
Answers to his present, future, and past.

"Why come to me?" he whispered low,
Seeking the reason for this shadowy show.
The raven replied, "For you seek the truth,
In the maze of life, in the cusp of youth."

"You're at a crossroads, choices to make,
Paths to tread, decisions at stake.
I've seen your struggles, felt your pain,

Watched you stand, time and again."
The raven's words, cryptic and deep,
Stirred memories, made the man weep.
For in its verse, he saw a reflection,
Of his own life, its imperfections.

"Seek the balance," the raven advised,
"Between heart and mind, be wise.
For life's journey is but a test,
To find oneself, amidst the rest."

The man nodded, taking the cue,
Realizing the raven's words were true.
For in its cryptic verse and tone,
Lay the wisdom, ancient and known.

As dawn approached, the raven took flight,
Leaving behind lessons, and the night.
The man, transformed, with newfound zest,
Thanked the raven, for its cryptic bequest.

For in that encounter, brief and profound,
He found guidance, a purpose unbound.
And with the raven's cryptic verse in heart,
He set forth, ready for a fresh start.

# Surgical Slumber's Nightmare

Within the cold confines of gleaming steel,
Where life's fragility seems all too real,
He rested, exposed to fate's cruel stare,
Lost in the grip of a chilling nightmare.

The scent of antiseptic, sharp and cold,
Whispered tales of procedures old.
The gleaming tools, aligned in rows,
Promised healing, yet also echoed woes.

His heart raced, a frantic beat,
As the surgical sheet covered his feet.
Voices murmured, distant and low,
As the anaesthesia began its slow tow.

Into the abyss, he started to slide,
A realm where reality and dreams collide.
Visions danced, twisted and strange,
As his consciousness began to rearrange.

He felt a pull, a tug deep within,
Awakening sensations, both dread and chagrin.
The scalpel's dance, precise and neat,
Yet he felt detached, from head to feet.

Echoes of voices, muffled and far,
Mingled with memories of a distant star.
Pain and relief, in a swirling blend,
As time and space seemed to bend.
Suddenly, a jolt, a piercing scream,
Ripped him away from the dream's regime.
Awareness returned, sharp and clear,
As the weight of reality drew near.

He felt the stitches, tight and neat,
The aftermath of the surgical feat.
Grateful for the skill, the care bestowed,
Yet haunted by the nightmare that flowed.

In the realm of recovery, time stood still,
As he grappled with the ordeal's chill.
For while the body heals, scars fade,
The mind remembers the price it paid.

With time and care, he'd rise again,
Stronger, resilient, free from pain.
But the memory of that surgical night,
Would forever cast a shadow, albeit slight.

# Sterile Lullabies

In the hushed corridors of cold despair,
Where machines hum and sterile air,
He found himself, amidst tubes and wires,
A captive of life's fragile fires.

The ICU, a realm of ghostly white,
Where day mingles indistinctly with night.
Monitors beeped, tracing life's fragile line,
As he lay there, suspended in time.

Around him, souls battled unseen foes,
Whispers of pain, silent throes.
Each bed held a story, a tale untold,
Of battles fierce, of spirits bold.

Yet, in this place of healing and hurt,
Where life dangles, fragile as dirt,
He felt the weight of a thousand sighs,
The silent pleas, the unanswered whys.

The nurse's touch, clinical and cold,
Yet a lifeline, a hand to hold.
The doctor's words, measured and few,
Promising hope, yet uncertainty too.

Beside him, an old man gasped for breath,
A dance with shadows, a flirt with death.
A young woman, with eyes that gleamed,
Held onto dreams, as life's thread seemed.

He heard the cries, the muffled sobs,
The prayers whispered to distant gods.
The hope that flickered, the despair that grew,
In this realm of sterile lullabies, where life's tapestry is rewoven anew.

And as the days blurred into endless night,
He felt himself drift, losing the fight.
The weight of solitude, the sting of tears,
The echoing silence, amplifying fears.

Yet, amidst the pain, a realization did creep,
That life, though fragile, is also deep.
For in these moments of despair and strife,
Lies the very essence, the core of life.

But as the darkness began to fold,
His spirit felt weary, his body old.
In the sterile lullabies of that place so grim,
He wondered if hope's light would ever dim.

# Mirror's Mockery

In a room dimly lit, a reflection stood still,
A face, a visage, a testament of will.
The glass, unyielding, captured every scar,
Every dream chased, every fallen star.

His eyes, once bright, now clouded with doubt,
Seeking answers to questions, the world left out.
The lines on his forehead, etched tales of yore,
Of battles fought, of dreams washed ashore.

The mirror bore witness to a soul's silent plea,
A yearning for acceptance, a desperate decree.
For in its depths, he saw not just a face,
But a chronicle of struggles, a dwindling grace.

The lips that once smiled, now curved in despair,
Whispering secrets to the vacant air.
The cheeks, once rosy, now pale and wan,
Telling tales of hopes, long gone.

Yet, in that reflection, a challenge arose,
A defiance against life's tumultuous throes.
For every scar, every tear, every line,
Spoke of resilience, of a spirit divine.

The mirror, though cold, held a truth profound,
That in every soul, strength is found.
Even when shadows of doubt creep near,
The heart's true essence remains clear.
But the weight of the world, its judgments and jeers,
Had left him questioning, after all these years.
Was he enough? Did he truly belong?
Or was he just a verse in life's tragic song?

And as he gazed, seeking solace and more,
The mirror's mockery echoed the lore.
Of a man seeking love, in a world so vast,
Hoping to reconcile with shadows of the past.

# Soliloquy of the Setting Sun

As dusk descends, shadows lengthen and merge,
Life's ballet unfolds, to a mournful dirge.
Golden rays retreat, as night's curtain drew,
Melding memories past, with promises anew.

Is life but a fleeting moment, a transient dream?
A blink in the vastness, a silent scream?
Yet, in that brief span, joy and sorrow intertwine,
Moments of despair, yet hope does shine.

The weight of regrets, heavy and profound,
Yet, the promise of tomorrow, a siren sound.
For every tear shed, a laughter does echo,
In the theatre of life, a continuous fresco.

Death, the final curtain, awaits us all,
But should that make our spirits small?
For in the dance of dusk and dawn,
Life's beauty and tragedy are drawn.

The inevitability of the end, a sombre song,
Yet, the journey's worth, the pull so strong.
To love, to lose, to dream, to dare,
In the face of the abyss, to still care.

For even as the night's darkness does descend,
Stars twinkle above, a celestial friend.
Reminding us, that even in the bleakest night,
Hope persists, a beacon of light.

So, in the twilight of life, as shadows grow long,
Remember the melody, the heart's eternal song.
For death may be certain, the end of the play,
But the dance of life, will forever sway.

# Elegy of Existence

Within the hush where reflections stir,
Where aspirations rise and memories blur,
A lone soul ponders his destined path,
While faultergeists murmur and phantoms' wrath.

The obsidian sky, pierced by starlight's gleam,
Holds tales of old, and futures unseen.
Yet, beneath its vastness, one can't help but feel,
The weight of existence, heavy and real.

Each pulse, a testament to life's fragile thread,
A dance between the living and the dread.
For in every corner, in shadow and light,
The faultergeists linger, ever so slight.

The trees, ancient sentinels, with secrets to tell,
Of love lost, battles fought, and heroes who fell.
Their leaves rustle with stories, both joyous and grim,
As faultergeists haunt the spaces between limb.

Rivers, those meandering paths of old,
Carry tales of adventures, legends retold.
Yet their waters hold more than just reflections clear,
For faultergeists lurk, preying on fear.

Mountains, majestic, with peaks so high,
Touching the heavens, kissing the sky.
But in their caverns, deep and profound,
Faultergeists' echoes are the only sound.

In cities bustling, where life never sleeps,
Among crowded lanes and alleys deep,
The laughter and tears, the hopes and the strife,
Are intertwined with faultergeists, sowing rife.

The heart, that fragile vessel of emotion,
Is a tumultuous, ever-churning ocean.
With waves of joy, and storms of sorrow,
Faultergeists ensure there's no clear morrow.

Yet, amidst this dance of shadow and light,
Where despair often overshadows the bright,
A resilient spirit, in humans does dwell,
Challenging faultergeists, breaking their spell.

For in the end, when all is said and done,
When the battle between hope and dread is won,
The essence of life, so intricate and vast,
Is the legacy we leave, the shadows we cast.

And as the final curtain begins to descend,
With faultergeists waiting, just around the bend,
One truth remains, clear and profound,
In love and memories, we are forever bound.

So, let not the faultergeists define the tale,
For human spirit, in the end, will prevail.
Though the journey is fraught with pain and strife,
Such is the exquisite melancholy of life.